HEPCAT

William Bramhall

Philomel Books · New York

For Hartley and Cabot, two cool cats.

Text and illustrations copyright © 2004 by William Bramhall.
All rights reserved. This book, or parts thereof, may not be reproduced
in any form without permission in writing from the publisher, Philomel Books,
a division of Penguin Young Readers Group, 345 Hudson Street, New York, NY 10014.
Philomel Books, Reg. U.S. Pat. & Tm. Off.
The scanning, uploading and distribution of this book via the Internet or
via any other means without the permission of the publisher is illegal and
punishable by law. Please purchase only authorized electronic editions,
and do not participate in or encourage electronic piracy of copyrighted materials.
Your support of the author's rights is appreciated.
Published simultaneously in Canada. Manufactured in China by South China
Printing Co. Ltd. Designed by Marikka Tamura. The text is set in Bokka.
The art for this book was created with crow quill pens, acrylic inks,
and watercolor washes on Bristol kid paper.
Library of Congress Cataloging-in-Publication Data
Bramhall, William. Hepcat / William Bramhall. p. cm.
Summary: Hepcat is suffering from stage fright until four beetles remind him
that music is everywhere and he ventures outside to find new inspiration.
[1. Stage fright–Fiction. 2. Rock music–Fiction. 3. cats–Fiction.] I. Title.
PZ7.B73573 He 2004 [E]–dc22 2003015976 ISBN 0-399-23896-4
1 3 5 7 9 10 8 6 4 2
First Impression

Hepcat was one nervous cat.
It was the night of his big concert!

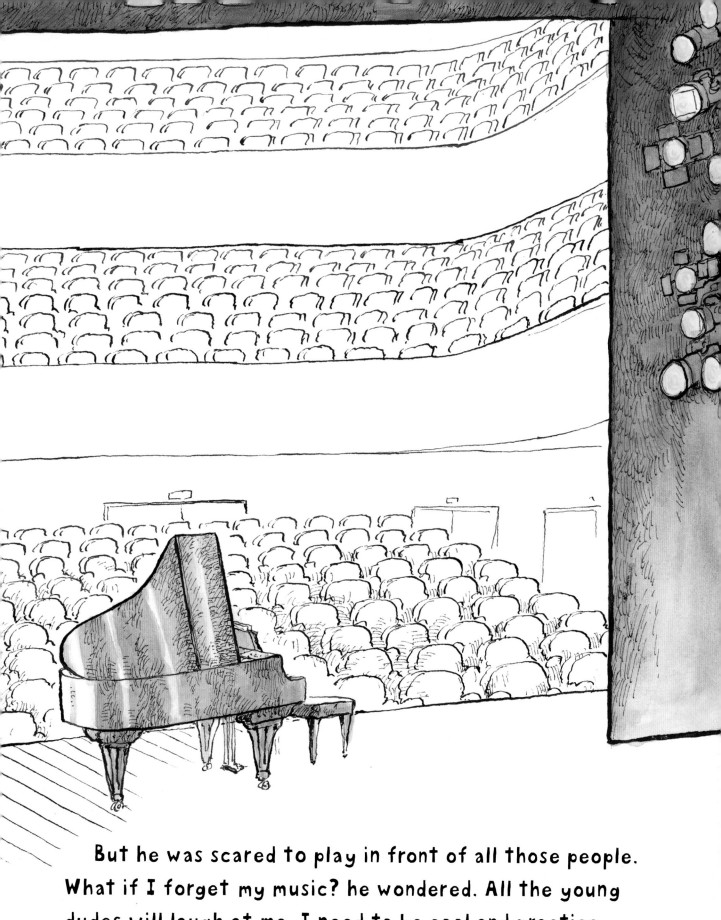

But he was scared to play in front of all those people.
What if I forget my music? he wondered. All the young
dudes will laugh at me. I need to be cool and practice
my tunes.

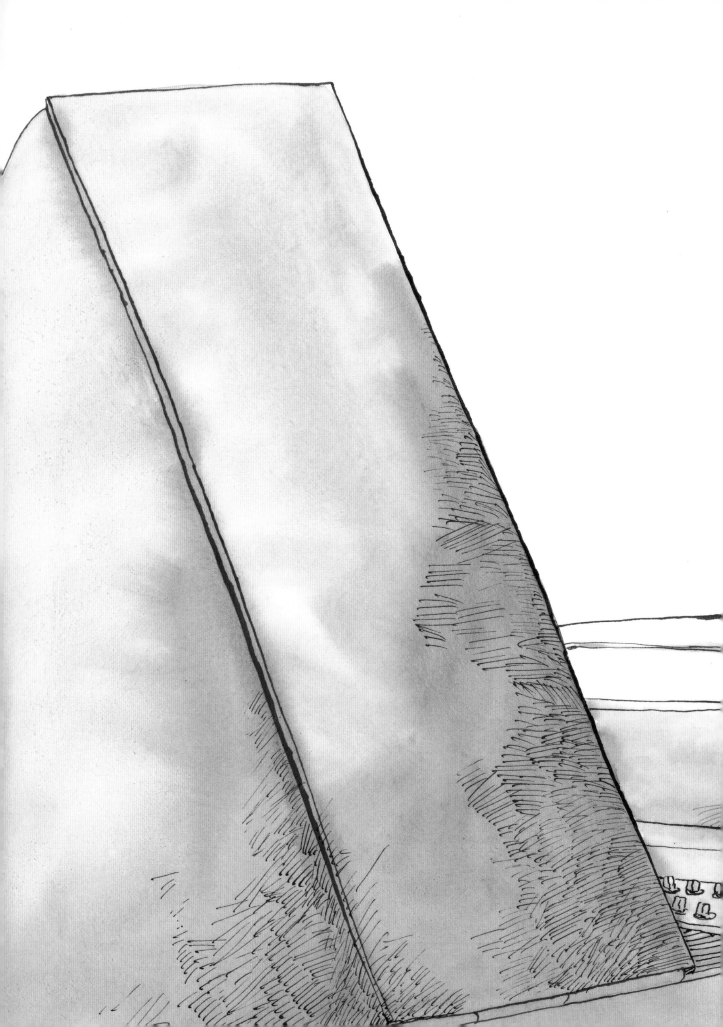

So Hepcat sat down at the ivories and tried to play.
But something was wrong—Hepcat had no music in him.
"I'm so nervous, I've lost my groove!" he shouted.

In the sudden silence, Hepcat heard music.
It was coming from the floor. . . .

He pulled up the floorboard and found four beetles
rocking out on guitar, bass, and drums.

"Help!" he said to the beetles. "My vibes have
vanished. I have a concert tonight and I'm one empty
jukebox."

"Hey, dude, don't make it bad," said one of the beetles.
"Take a sad song and make it better."

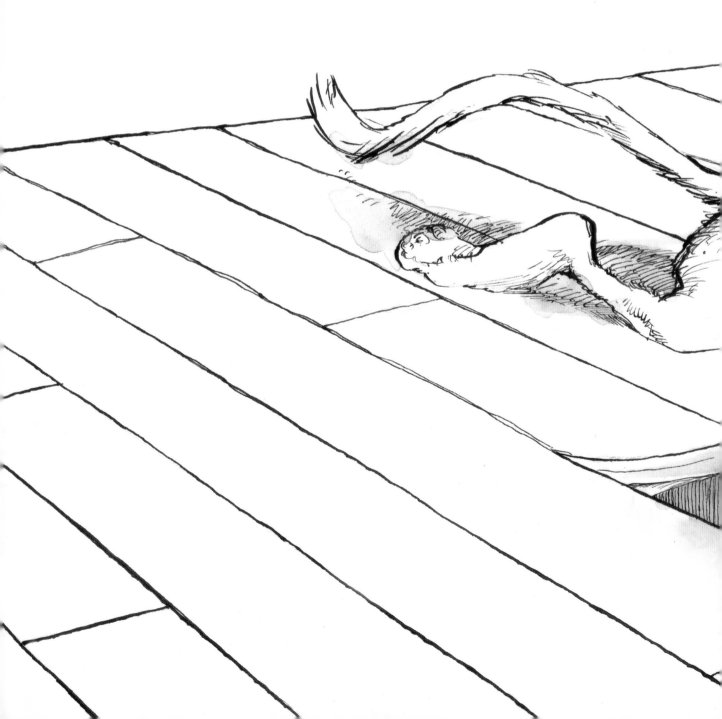

Hepcat was confused. "Say what?" he asked.
"Just cruise the scene, man,"
said the beetle. "Music is EVERYwhere."

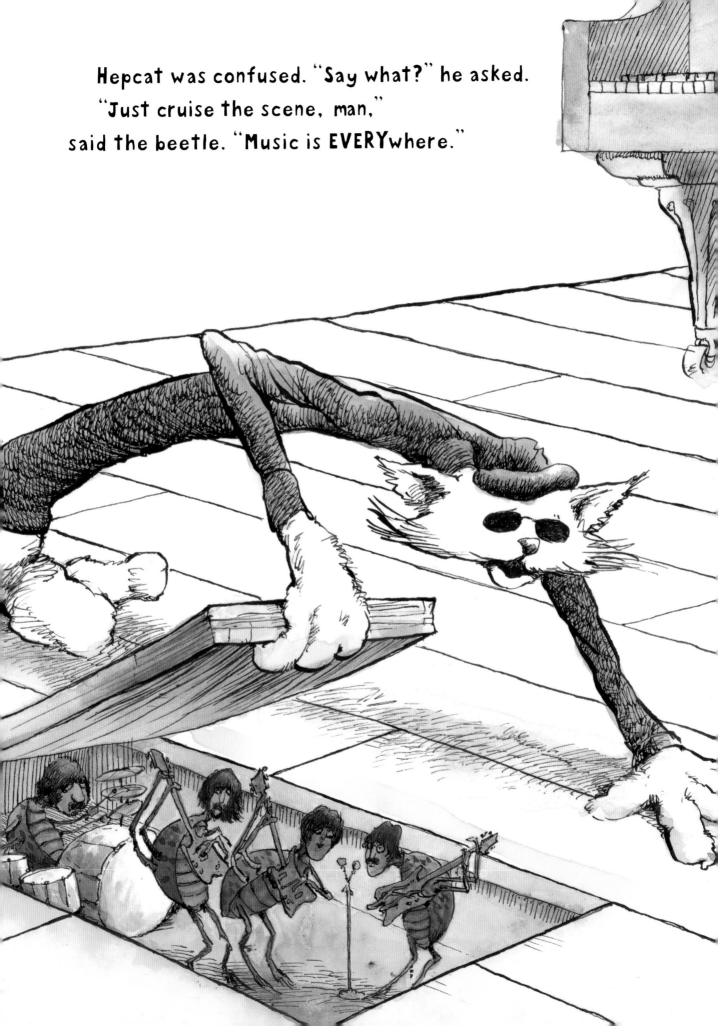

So Hepcat bopped outside. The wind blew cold and
the clouds were growing thick. He passed a lonely hound
dog on the street, telling sad tales on his harmonica.

Hepcat wanted to ask him if there was any music
nearby, but the hound dog was too busy feeling the blues.
"Blue's not my color," Hepcat said.

Hepcat motored to the busy street. Horns beeped, sirens wailed, trains went clackety-clack and woooo-woo. A car screeched past. "Whoa, be good, Johnny!" Hepcat shouted. "How's a cat supposed to hear music with all this racket going on?" But the traffic just danced on by, swaying and pulsing to its own crazy beat.

"Out of here," said Hepcat.

Hepcat climbed a tree, where he found two lovebirds cooing among the leaves. "What's the word, birds? Any tunes up here for a cat to scratch?" But the lovebirds were too busy whistling to hear. "Love may be all YOU need," Hepcat said, "but I need a melody or three."

He tried the pond next. But all he found was a frog croaking up a storm. "Good golly, Miss Molly!" he said. "Somebody put a frog down that frog's throat. I can't hear a thing."

The wind was blowing hard now.
Dark clouds rumbled and grumbled,
BOOM, BOOM—kettledrums pounding
in the sky. "Yikes!" said Hepcat.
"I'd better quit this scene!"

Rain poured down, chii chii chii-chii—
snare drums rattling, cymbals crashing.
Hepcat was one soggy feline.

Then came the biggest gust of all. Clarinets and saxophones blew their lips off. A giant accordion picked up Hepcat and squeezed him in and out, in and out. "Easy, squeezies! Put me down!"

Hepcat landed on top of a clock tower. "Uh-oh—eight o'clock! It's time for my concert and I still haven't found any—"

Suddenly the big brass bells rang and clanged. So did Hepcat's head. And that's when he finally heard it. The beeping horns, the whistling birds. The kettledrum thunder, the woodwind breeze.

"Well, I'll be a ding-dong daddy-o! The beetles were right. Music IS everywhere!

"Ca-raa-zy, man!"
Hepcat was so happy, he let the wind carry him all the way to the concert hall . . .

. . . where he riffed and rocked, jumped and jived, giving the best performance of his life.

And for one night, Hepcat truly was
the coolest cat in town.